For my two wolves
L.B.

For Tommy, Priscilla and Andy
M.D.

MYRIAD BOOKS LIMITED
35 Bishopsthorpe Road, London SE26 4PA

First published in 1999 by
MIJADE PUBLICATIONS
16-18, rue de l'Ouvrage
5000 Namur-Belgium

ISBN 1 84746 108 5
EAN 978 1 84746 108 7

Printed in China

Laurence Bourguignon   Michaël Derullieux

BIG WOLF'S
Magic Tricks

MYRIAD BOOKS LIMITED

Big Wolf has just returned home after a long walk in the woods.

He opens his front door then stops suddenly.

"Someone has been in my house again, I can smell them!"

he growls in a big voice.

He searches the whole house.

He even looks under the bed.

But he can't find anyone. Big Wolf is very angry.

"Tomorrow, instead of going for a walk in the woods,

I'll stay here and hide.

I'll soon see who comes into my house when I'm away."

The next morning Big Wolf climbs into his
cooking pot.
Very soon he hears a rustling noise, then
a footstep. The door opens with a creak.
Slowly Big Wolf peeps out from the pot.
And what does he see?
A rabbit! A plump, white rabbit sitting reading
his newspaper and drinking
from a straw!

"How nice of you to come and visit me!" shouts Big Wolf, leaping out of the pot.
"You're staying for dinner I hope?"

The plump rabbit rolls his eyes.
"Wait, Mister Wolf, don't hurt me!
I'm no ordinary rabbit you know!"

"Oh really? When I look at you
All I see is a good rabbit stew!"
says Big Wolf.

"It would be a big mistake to eat me!" says the rabbit. Suddenly the rabbit pushes a pack of cards up in front of him. "Come on, choose one, choose any card," he says to Big Wolf. Big Wolf picks a card and puts it back into the pack.

The rabbit starts shuffling the cards
at breathtaking speed.
"And here is your card!"
the rabbit shouts.
"Fantastic!" Big Wolf exclaims.
"How did you do that?"

"I told you. I'm no ordinary rabbit.
In fact, I'm a magician rabbit but please,
don't tell anyone! Nobody should know!"

From that moment Big Wolf and
Magician Rabbit become firm friends.
In the long winter evenings Magician
Rabbit entertained Big Wolf
with jokes and card tricks.

But as the weather got warmer, Magician Rabbit
became quite sad.

He lost his appetite. He couldn't sleep.
He didn't even feel like doing card tricks anymore.
"I think I would like to get married," he sighed.

"I can find you a wife," Big Wolf said.
That night, he went out into the wood
and returned with a pretty lady rabbit.

Magician Rabbit and the pretty lady rabbit fell in love straight away and were very happy. Big Wolf was happy too.

Soon the house filled up with little rabbits.

For the first time in his life, Big Wolf could enjoy the simple pleasures of family life.

Big Wolf's favourite time was in the evening when he sat down
in his armchair and opened up his big story book.
All the young rabbits would gather around with their ears pricked up.

"Which story do you want tonight?" he would ask, and every evening the young rabbits gave the same answer. "Tell us the story of the Wolf and Magician Rabbit," they would say.
So Big Wolf closed his book and told them the story...

But out in the forest, news travels fast. One morning as Big Wolf is on his way home with his shopping a pack of wolves suddenly blocks his way. "Look who's here! Isn't it our dear friend Big Wolf?" says the leader of the pack.

"Aren't we invited to have Christmas dinner at your place?
I hope rabbit is going to be on the menu!"
Before Big Wolf can speak, the leader shouts out,
"It is so nice of you to have thought of us!
We'll see you on Christmas Day!"

Big Wolf runs back home.

"We are lost!" he shouts and he tells Magician Rabbit the whole story.

"You don't need to worry," his friend says. "You forget I am no ordinary rabbit. I've got more than one trick up my sleeve! Let's set up a nice Christmas tree and welcome your friends!"

The big day finally arrives.
At one o'clock sharp,
the wolves knock at the door.
"It's us! Merry Christmas Big Wolf!"

"Merry Christmas my friends!
Please come in
and make yourselves at home.
We were waiting for you
before we started cooking..."

"It will soon be ready," Big Wolf
assures them and puts the pot
full of rabbits on to boil.
"In the meantime I've prepared
a little something just for you."
Big Wolf pulls a pack of cards out
of his pocket. "Come on! Choose
a card, any card," he says.

Big Wolf is well trained and he can shuffle the cards at breathtaking speed. His guests are so spellbound that they don't see the rabbit family slowly escape from the pot one by one.

At long last one of the guests remembers. "Didn't we come to eat some rabbit stew?"
Big Wolf lifts the lid on the pot but all they can see is dirty black water.
"What a disaster!" Big Wolf exclaims. "I've always been a bad cook."

A bad cook maybe, but a very good magician!